One by One

GARTH PIG'S RAIN SONG

by **MARY RAYNER**

Dutton Children's Books • New York

Copyright © 1994 by Mary Rayner
All rights reserved.

CIP Data is available.

First published in the United States 1994 by Dutton Children's Books,
a division of Penguin Books USA Inc., 375 Hudson Street, New York, New York 10014.
Originally published in Great Britain 1994 by Macmillan Children's Books, London.
Typography by Adrian Leichter
Printed in Singapore   First American Edition
1 3 5 7 9 10 8 6 4 2
ISBN 0-525-45240-0

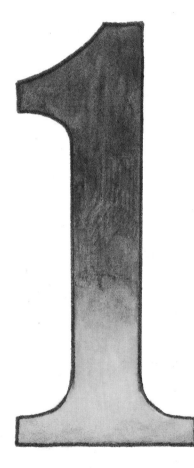

The piglets are marching one by one,
Hurrah! Hurrah!
The piglets are marching one by one,
Hurrah! Hurrah!
The piglets are marching one by one,
Garth Pig has stopped and is eating a bun,
And they all go marching,
For to get out of the rain.

The piglets are marching two by two,
Hurrah! Hurrah!
The piglets are marching two by two,
Hurrah! Hurrah!
The piglets are marching two by two,
Benjamin finds something better to do,
And they all go marching,
For to get out of the rain.

The piglets are marching three by three,
    Hurrah! Hurrah!
The piglets are marching three by three,
    Hurrah! Hurrah!
The piglets are marching three by three,
Toby has stopped and is climbing a tree,
And they all go marching,
For to get out of the rain.

The piglets are marching four by four,
 Hurrah! Hurrah!
The piglets are marching four by four,
 Hurrah! Hurrah!
The piglets are marching four by four,
Alun is knocking on *somebody's* door,
And they all go marching,
For to get out of the rain.

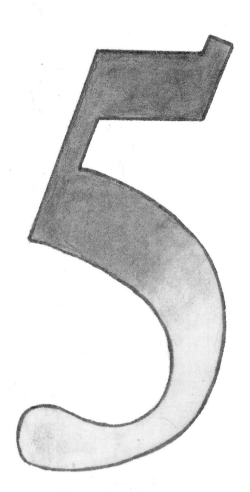

The piglets are marching five by five,
    Hurrah! Hurrah!
The piglets are marching five by five,
    Hurrah! Hurrah!
The piglets are marching five by five,
Cindy discovers some bees in a hive,
And they all go marching,
For to get out of the rain.

The piglets are marching six by six,
    Hurrah! Hurrah!
The piglets are marching six by six,
    Hurrah! Hurrah!
The piglets are marching six by six,
Wicked young William is up to his tricks,
And they all go marching,
For to get out of the rain.

The piglets are marching seven by seven,
　　Hurrah! Hurrah!
The piglets are marching seven by seven,
　　Hurrah! Hurrah!
The piglets are marching seven by seven,
Hilary's going as high up as Heaven,
And they all go marching,
For to get out of the rain.

The piglets are marching eight by eight,

    Hurrah! Hurrah!

The piglets are marching eight by eight,

    Hurrah! Hurrah!

The piglets are marching eight by eight,

Sarah is swinging on somebody's gate,

And they all go marching,

For to get out of the rain.

The piglets are marching nine by nine,
    Hurrah! Hurrah!
The piglets are marching nine by nine,
    Hurrah! Hurrah!
The piglets are marching nine by nine,
Sorrel is leading them all in a line,
And they all go marching,
For to get out of the rain.

The piglets are marching ten by ten,
Hurrah! Hurrah!
The piglets are marching ten by ten,
Hurrah! Hurrah!
The piglets are marching ten by ten,

If you want any more, you can sing it again,

And they all ran back home . . .

For to get out of the rain.

PjRAY   Rayner, Mary
            One by one
            476815

$5.99

DATE			